DINOSAUR
ROAR!

For John Smith

PUFFIN BOOKS
Published by the Penguin Group
Penguin Young Readers Group, 345 Hudson Street, New York, New York 10014, U.S.A.
Penguin Group (Canada), 90 Eglinton Avenue East, Suite 700, Toronto, Ontario,
Canada M4P 2Y3 (a division of Pearson Penguin Canada Inc.)
Penguin Books Ltd, 80 Strand, London WC2R 0RL, England
Penguin Ireland, 25 St Stephen's Green, Dublin 2, Ireland
(a division of Penguin Books Ltd)
Penguin Group (Australia), 250 Camberwell Road, Camberwell, Victoria 3124, Australia
(a division of Pearson Australia Group Pty Ltd)
Penguin Books India Pvt Ltd, 11 Community Centre, Panchsheel Park, New Delhi - 110 017, India
Penguin Group (NZ), 67 Apollo Drive, Rosedale, North Shore 0632, New Zealand
(a division of Pearson New Zealand Ltd)
Penguin Books (South Africa) (Pty) Ltd, 24 Sturdee Avenue,
Rosebank, Johannesburg 2196, South Africa

Registered Offices: Penguin Books Ltd, 80 Strand, London WC2R 0RL, England

First published in Great Britain by Ragged Bears Limited, Hampshire, England, 1994
First published in the United States of America by Dutton Children's Books,
a member of Penguin Putnam Inc., 1994
Published by Puffin Books, a division of Penguin Putnam Books for Young Readers, 2001
This edition published by Puffin Books, a division of Penguin Young Readers Group, 2009

12

Text copyright © Henrietta Stickland, 1994
Illustrations copyright © Paul Stickland, 1994
All rights reserved

THE LIBRARY OF CONGRESS HAS CATALOGED THE DUTTON CHILDREN'S BOOKS EDITION AS FOLLOWS:
Stickland, Paul.
Dinosaur roar! / by Paul and Henrietta Stickland.—1st American ed.
p. cm.
Summary: Illustrations and rhyming text present all kinds of dinosaurs,
including ones that are sweet, grumpy, spiky, or lumpy.
ISBN: 0-525-45276-1 (hc)
[1. Dinosaurs—Fiction. 2. Stories in rhyme.] I. Stickland, Henrietta. II. Title.
PZ8.3.S854Di 1994 [E]—dc20 93-43959 CIP AC

Puffin Books ISBN 978-0-14-056808-0

Manufactured in China

DINOSAUR ROAR!

PAUL & HENRIETTA STICKLAND

PUFFIN BOOKS
An Imprint of Penguin Group (USA) Inc.

Dinosaur roar,

dinosaur squeak,

dinosaur fierce,

dinosaur meek,

dinosaur fast,

dinosaur slow,

dinosaur above

and dinosaur below.

Dinosaur weak,

dinosaur strong,

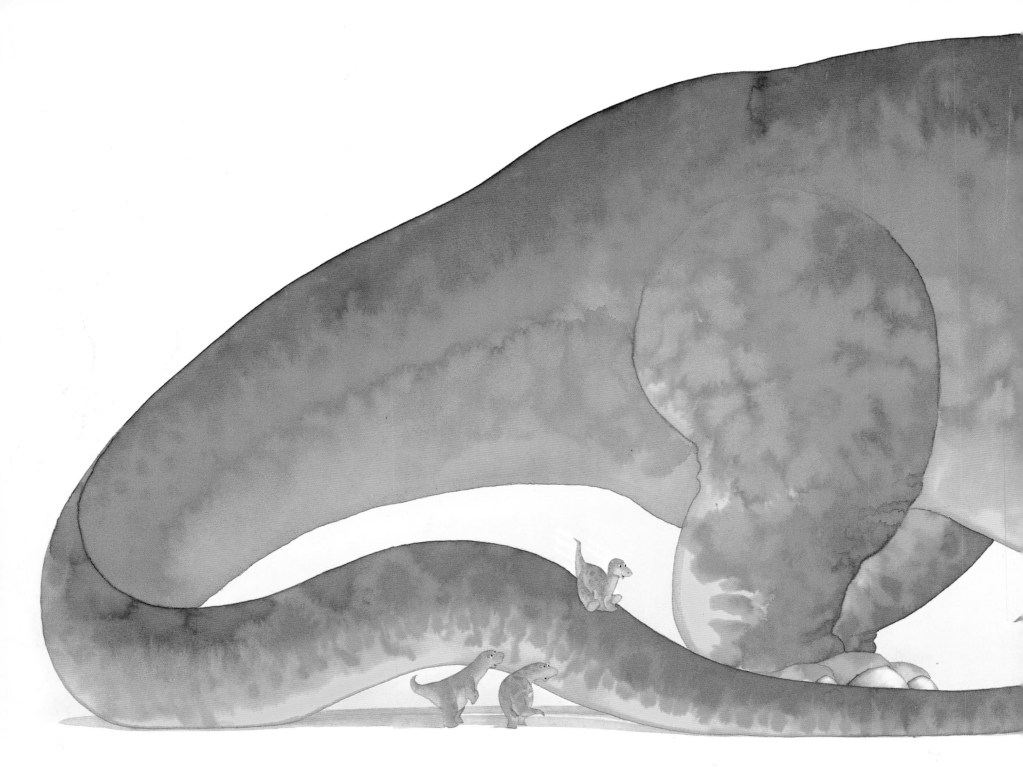

dinosaur short

or very, very long.

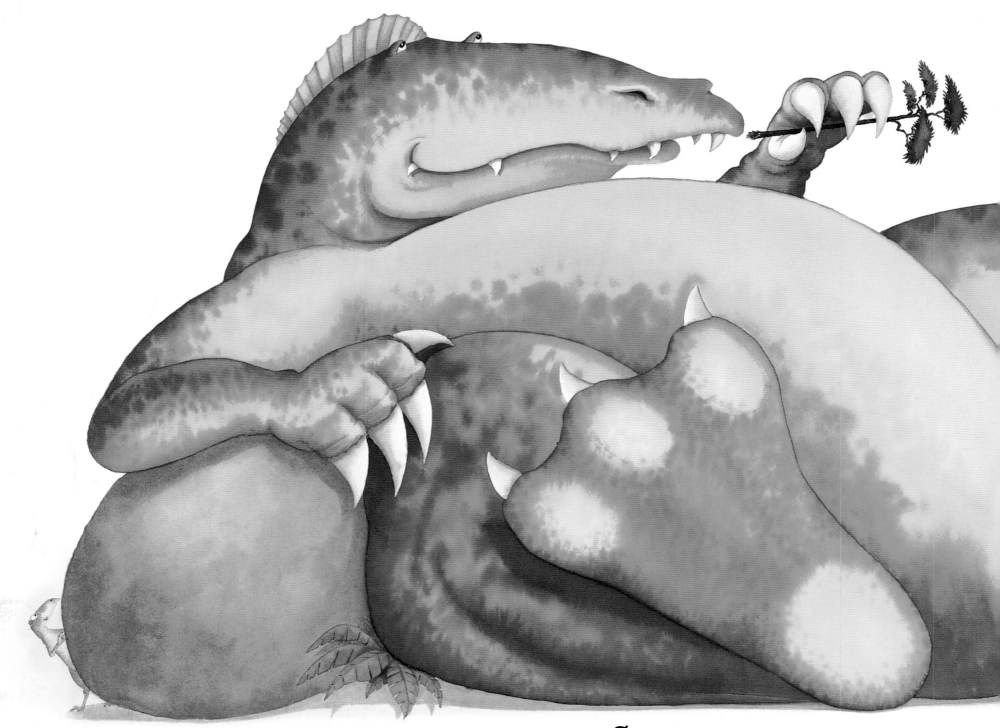

Dinosaur fat,

dinosaur tiny,

dinosaur clean

and dinosaur slimy.

Dinosaur sweet,

dinosaur grumpy,

dinosaur spiky

and dinosaur lumpy.

All sorts of dinosaurs

eating up their lunch,

gobble, gobble, nibble, nibble,

munch, munch, scrunch!

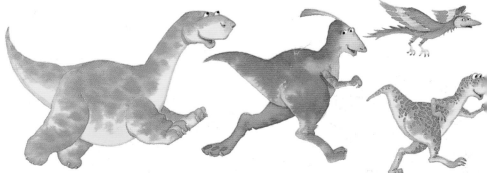

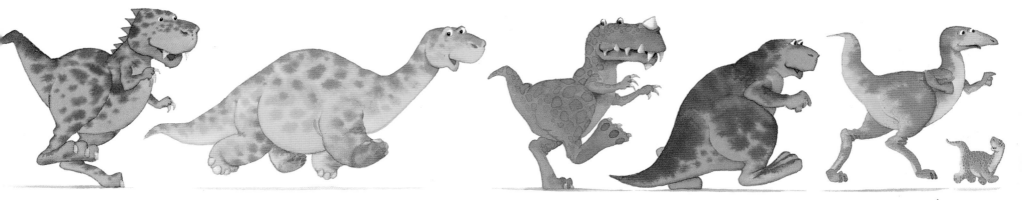